ONE STEP, TWO...

ONE STEP, TWO...

by Charlotte Zolotow
pictures by Cindy Wheeler

Lothrop, Lee & Shepard Books
New York

Text copyright © 1955, 1981 by Charlotte Zolotow
Illustrations copyright © 1981 by Cindy Wheeler

Library of Congress Cataloging in Publication Data

Zolotow, Charlotte Shapiro, (date)   One step, two...
Summary: While out for a walk on a spring morning, a little girl shows her mother things grown-ups sometimes miss. [1. Spring—Fiction. 2. Mothers and daughters —Fiction] I. Wheeler, Cindy. II. Title. PZ7.Z770n 1980   [E]   80-11749   ISBN 0-688-41971-2   ISBN 0-688-51971-7 (lib. bdg.)

Once again, for Cres

ne spring morning, the mother and her little
girl came down the steps of their house—one
step, two steps, three steps—and they were
down. They started to walk to the corner.

"See that!" said the little girl.

"What?" asked the mother.

And then she saw—a yellow crocus shining in the grass.

One step, two steps, three steps more.

"Come," said the mother.

But the little girl stood still.

"Look!" she said.

The mother looked, and then she saw it too—
a fat gray cat prowling through the bushes next
door.

One step, two steps, three steps, four—and the little girl stopped again.

"See *that!*" she said, and pointed to a blue bird floating down to earth with its white-tipped wings spread wide.

One step, two … three, four, five steps—and
six. The little girl stooped down, and picked up a
round white pebble that gleamed in the sun like
a little pale moon.

One, two, three, four, five, six, seven steps.

"See!" said the little girl.

And her mother saw the dresses and pants and towels dancing on the line.

One, two, three, four, five, six, seven, eight, nine steps.

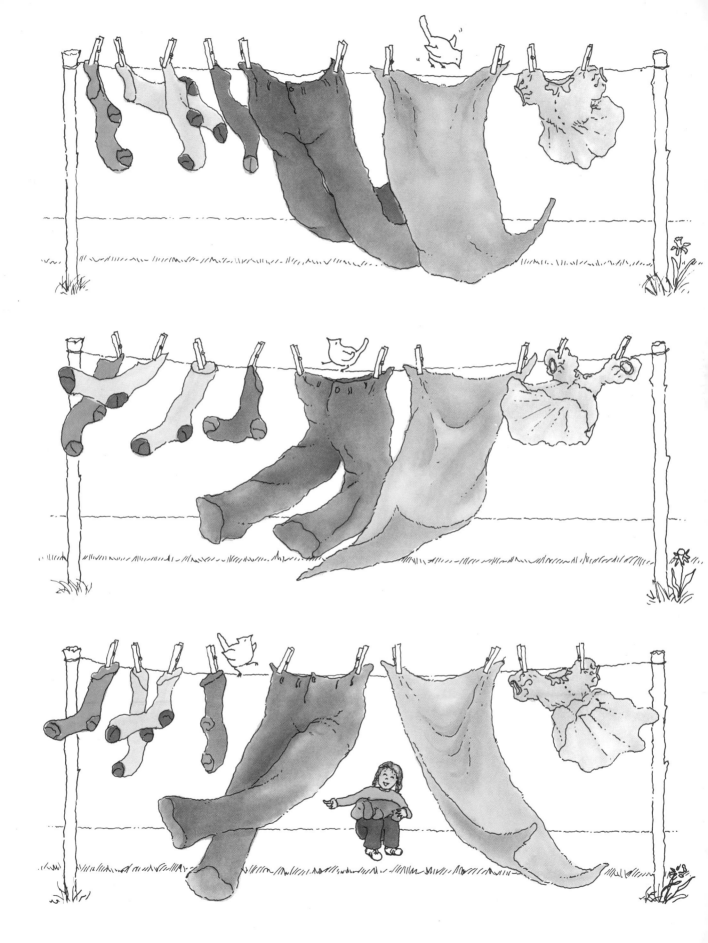

GrnnnGRRRRRNNNNNNNDDDDDDDDD!
"Hear that!" the little girl shouted.

The garbage man across the street was grinding up the garbage he'd thrown into the truck.

One, two, three, four, five, six, seven, eight, nine, ten, eleven...

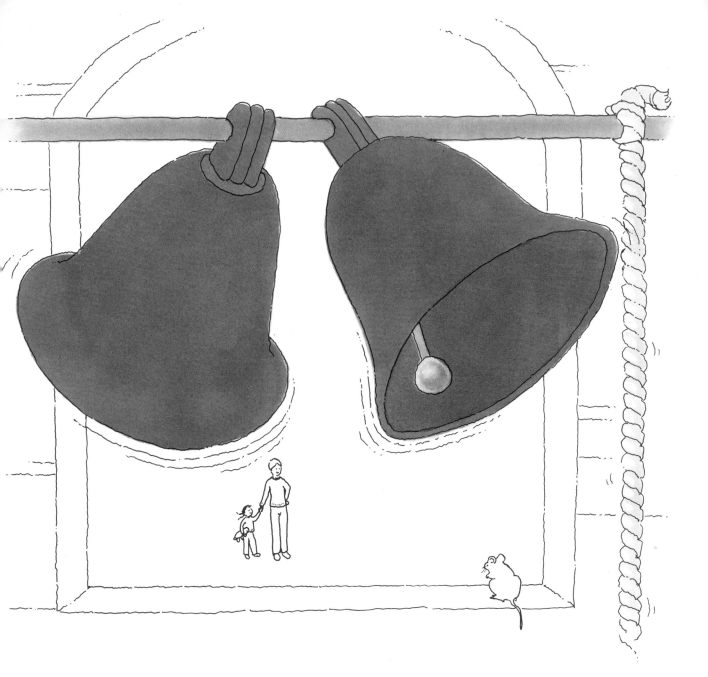

Suddenly the bells of the church burst into music like a flock of birds in the sky. The little girl took her mother's hand and stood still and listened until they stopped ringing.

Then she went on.

One, two, three, four, five, six, seven, eight, nine, ten, eleven, and twelve...

They had reached the end of the block.
"Truck," said the little girl as the school bus
whished by.

"Lunchtime," said the mother. She took her little girl's hand and they started home.

One, two, three, four, five, six steps toward home.

The little girl bent down to pick some daffodils swelling yellow on their flat stems.

"No," said her mother, "they are not ours. But you may smell them."

When the little girl stood up, she smiled at her mother and her nose was tipped with yellow powder.

One, two, three, four, five, six, seven...

The little girl stopped and her eyes grew round.

"How do," said Mr. Peabody. And Mr. Peabody's big dog wagged his tail and licked the yellow daffodil powder off the little girl's nose.

One, two, three, four, five, six, seven, eight,
nine, ten—

They passed a house with plants in the
window.

"Pretty!" said the little girl.

"Yes," agreed her mother. "Red geraniums."

One, two, three, four, five, six, seven, eight,
nine, ten, e-l-e-v-e-n, t-w-e-l-v-e…

"Home again!" said the mother as they turned
up the walk to their house.
    But at the stairs the little girl stopped.

"Up," she said, reaching with both arms.
Her mother gathered her up and hugged her
close.

"What a lovely walk, and what a lot of things
we saw. Thank you for showing me—
    the blue jay in the sky,
    the gray cat prowling by,
    the yellow crocus in the grass,
    the garbage truck, the daffodils,
    the little pebble like a moon,
    the lovely bells that rang at noon."

But the little girl didn't hear. She was fast asleep.

CHARLOTTE ZOLOTOW, Editorial Director and Associate Publisher of Harper Junior Books, is the author of over sixty books for children, including *Sleepy Book* and *A Tiger Called Thomas* on the Lothrop list.

Mrs. Zolotow was born in Norfolk, Virginia, and attended the University of Wisconsin. She lives in Hastings-on-Hudson, New York.

CINDY WHEELER makes her Lothrop debut with the revised edition of *One Step, Two....* She received her BFA from Auburn University in Alabama and now works as a full-time freelance illustrator. Ms. Wheeler lives in Garrison, New York. Working on this book was especially enjoyable to the artist because "it reminds us that some of the most miraculous things in life happen day after day right in our backyard."

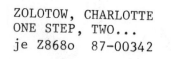